THE
RED BRICK LIBRARY
CONTEST
WRITE
THE
BEST STORY
AND WIN
FIRST PRIZE:
A RIDE ON THE SOOPER
DOOPER LOOPER ROLLER
COASTER WITH
ANNE MILES
AUTHOR OF
THE RUNAWAY ROLLER
COASTER

The Red Brick Library was having a contest: Write the best story. Win first prize.

First prize was a ride on the Sooper Dooper Looper roller coaster with my favorite author, Anne Miles, who wrote *The Runaway Roller Coaster*.

Wow! First prizes don't get any better than that.

I ran home.
Went to my room.
Shut the door.
I sharpened five pencils.
Opened my notebook to a brand-new page.
And thought.
And thought.
And thought.
And all I could think was this writing stuff was hard and lonely.
Maybe I needed help.

The Best Story

Eileen Spinelli

ILLUSTRATIONS BY

Anne Wilsdorf

SCHOLASTIC INC.
New York Toronto London Auckland
Sydney Mexico City New Delhi Hong Kong

For my story pals
Jan Powell and
Ellen and Ralph Nathan
—ES

To Jeanne Barbier
—AW

ISBN: 978-0-545-23698-0

Text copyright © 2008 by Eileen Spinelli. Illustrations copyright © 2008 by Anne Wilsdorf. All rights reserved. Published by Scholastic Inc., 557 Broadway, New York, NY 10012, by arrangement with Dial Books for Young Readers, a division of Penguin Young Readers Group, a member of Penguin Group (USA) Inc. SCHOLASTIC and associated logos are trademarks and/or registered trademarks of Scholastic Inc.

12 11 10 9 8 7 6 5 4 3 2 1   10 11 12 13 14 15/0

Printed in the U.S.A.   40

First Scholastic printing, January 2010

Designed by Lily Malcom
Text set in Sabon
The art was created using watercolor and China ink on white paper.

I told my brother Tim about the contest.
"The best stories," said my brother Tim, "have lots of action."

So I wrote a lot of action into my story.

I wrote about a bus hurtling down the highway
with no one at the wheel.

I added a tornado.

And a pirate.

And a great white shark.

But the story didn't seem quite right.

So I asked my dad and he said, "The best stories have plenty of humor."

So I changed the great white shark to a monkey.
And I put the monkey at the wheel of the bus.
And I turned the tornado into turnips.
And I dressed the pirate in polka-dotted pajamas.

Dad laughed so hard he popped a shirt button.
Even so, this story didn't feel quite right either.

Along came Aunt Jane. "What are you doing?" she asked.

"I'm writing a story. The *best* story. For a contest at the library. I can win a roller coaster ride with my favorite author!"

"Oh, well then," said Aunt Jane. "Here's all you need to know—the best stories are the ones that make people cry."

So I gave the bus a flat tire.
I sent the monkey to the funeral of his pet goldfish.
I turned the turnips into onions.
And I made the pirate chop every one.
There were lots of tears.
But the story still wasn't right.

My teenage cousin Anika said, "I have news for you—
if it's not romantic it's a loser."

So the pirate introduced the monkey to his sister Grace.
And they fell in love.
And I turned the onions into wedding invitations.
And everyone lived happily ever after.

Finally my story was ready, so I read it to my family.

"Not enough action," said my brother Tim.

"Maybe the monkey can fall into the wedding cake," said Dad. "That would really be funny."

"It's hard to cry at a wedding when the groom is a monkey," said Aunt Jane.

Anika said it would be perfect if I added a kiss.

In all this time my mother hadn't said a word. So I asked her:
"What do you think is the best story?"

She gave me a hug. "I think the best story is one that comes from the heart. Your own heart."

That night, after supper, I looked into my own heart.
And rewrote my story.
   No more monkey.
   No more pirate.
   No more wedding invitations.
   No more "happily ever after."

My new best story is about my family.
And my two best friends Tara and Josh.
It's about my cat Ollie, who sleeps on his back.
And snow days.
And toast with strawberry jam.
It's about fireworks.
And rainbows.
And bike rides.

My biggest problem was keeping the story short. Once I
started pulling things out of my heart it was hard to stop.
When my story was finished, I turned it in to the judges.

Maybe I'll win that roller coaster ride with Anne Miles and maybe I won't.

Either way, I'll be happy. I'll be a winner.

Because the story I wrote is my own.

Not somebody else's.

And that makes it the best.